Cat Chocolate

Written by Kate Darling
Illustrated by Mitch Vane

An easy-to-read SOLO
for beginning readers

Scholastic Canada Ltd.
New York Toronto London Auckland Sydney
Mexico City New Delhi Hong Kong

Scholastic Canada Ltd.
175 Hillmount Road, Markham, Ontario, Canada L6C 1Z7

Scholastic Inc.
555 Broadway, New York, NY 10012, USA

Scholastic Australia Pty Limited
PO Box 579, Gosford, NSW 2250, Australia

Scholastic New Zealand Limited
Private Bag 94407, Greenmount, Auckland, New Zealand

Scholastic Ltd.
Villiers House, Clarendon Avenue, Leamington Spa,
Warwickshire CV32 5PR, UK

First published by Omnibus Books, part of the
SCHOLASTIC GROUP, Sydney, Australia.

National Library of Canada Cataloguing in Publication Data
Darling, Kate
  Cat chocolate
(Solo reading)
ISBN 0-439-98884-5
  I. Vane, Mitch II. Title. III. Series.
PZ7.D29Ca 2002   j823   2001-900548-2

5 4 3 2 1   Printed and bound in Canada.   1 2 3 4 / 0

For Beau, to read on the bus – K.D.

For Danny, Talia and Jordie – M.V.

Note to Readers:
Never give chocolate to a cat, dog, or other
animal. Pets should only be given pet treats.

Chapter 1

Most cats like fish or milk or chopped-up meat. But not Chester. Chester was not like other cats. Chester was spoiled rotten, and he loved it.

He loved his owner, Tina.

He loved sleeping in the sun.

He loved being the only cat in the house.

But most of all, he loved chocolate treats. Tina could make him do almost anything for one chocolate treat.

One morning, Tina found
Chester asleep on the spare bed.
He was dreaming of chocolate
frogs hopping into his mouth.

Tina woke him up. She had put a chocolate treat on his pillow.

"Chester," she said in a sweet voice, "there's something I have to tell you."

Chester's tail twitched. He didn't like the sound of this.

"My cousin Ken is coming to stay and he will have to sleep in this bed. Isn't that good news? We will have a friend to play with."

Chester's tail twitched and his
ears lay back against his head. He
did *not* think it was good news.
This was the best and warmest
spot in the house.

"Don't be angry. You can sleep in the kitchen." Tina pushed the chocolate treat under his nose and got up. "Be happy, Chester," she said.

But Chester was not happy at all.

Chapter 2

When Ken arrived, Chester hid under the bed. He saw Tina's two feet in her red sandals, and next to them two strange feet in black shoes.

Tina tried to get Chester to
come out, but he would not move.
She stuck her head under the
bed. "Please, Chester," she said.
"Say hello to Ken."

Chester didn't want to say hello
to a bed-stealer.

Ken bent down and stuck out a skinny white hand to pat Chester.

Chester's tail flicked like a snake. He hissed at Ken, and Ken jumped back.

Tina was angry. She told Chester to be nice, but he just hissed again.

"Fine, then." Tina stamped her foot. "Stay there all day if you like."

She turned to Ken. "Do you like chocolate?" she asked in a very loud voice. "Mum has just made a chocolate cake."

"Oh yes," said Ken. He licked his lips. "I *love* chocolate."

Chester didn't like the sound of *that* one bit.

"I'll have three slices," said Ken.

What a pig! Chester wanted to jump out and bite Ken on the leg, but he waited where he was until the children had left.

When he came out at last, there
was no cake left. Ken had eaten
it all!

Chapter 3

On the second day of Ken's visit, Tina found Chester asleep in the kitchen. He was dreaming of chocolate mice running into his mouth.

Tina wanted Chester to play tea parties in the clubhouse with her and Ken.

"Come on," she said.

Chester kept his eyes shut.

"There's a soft cushion in the clubhouse for you, and a surprise!" Chester's ear twitched.

"I saved the last chocolate brownie for you. Please come and play." Tina stroked his fur, and Chester began to purr. He *loved* chocolate brownies.

Chester let Tina carry him down
the backyard to the clubhouse. The
first thing he saw there was Ken.

He was sitting on the soft cushion, and the last bit of chocolate brownie was in his mouth.

"Mmm," said Ken, with his mouth full. "Thanks for the brownie. That was very yummy."

Chester jumped down and ran away. He was very, very angry. He hid under the car and didn't come out all afternoon.

Chapter 4

On the third day of Ken's visit the sky was grey. Ken and Tina decided to go outside and look for worms and snails.

Tina asked Chester if he wanted to come.

Chester turned his head away
and started to lick his back leg.
He wasn't going anywhere with
that horrid boy!

The two children put on their
warm coats and went outside.

Chester closed his eyes and began to dream about chocolate worms, all slithering and sliding into his mouth.

28

When he woke up again, he
needed to go outside.
He squeezed through the
cat door.

It was raining outside. Chester
hated to get wet. He dashed for
the garden and found a nice dry
place under a bush.

When he had finished, he ran back to his cat door as fast as he could. The rain was falling harder.

His cat door was blocked with
something too heavy to move!

Chester began to make a lot of
noise. He could smell hot chocolate
inside. Tina and Ken must be in
there, drinking big mugs of yummy
chocolate, while he was stuck in
the rain getting soaking wet.

Chester wailed even louder.

Tina opened the door.

"Oh you poor thing!" She picked him up and carried him inside. "Ken put a box in front of your door to keep the wind out. He's very sorry."

Chester looked at Ken.

Ken was finishing off a huge mug of hot chocolate. He didn't look sorry at all.

Chapter 5

Late that night, Chester heard
someone at the kitchen door. He
opened one eye. It was Ken.

Chester sat still in the shadows and watched.

Ken tiptoed into the kitchen.
He went to the counter and
opened the cake tin. There was
no chocolate cake in there.

He looked inside the cookie jar. There were no chocolate brownies left.

He opened the tin of chocolate
drink mix. That was empty too.

Way up high he found a small
box. He got it down.

Ken sniffed the box. "Yum! This smells like chocolate."

He opened it
and tasted what
was inside.

"Great! It *is* chocolate."

Chester's whiskers twitched, but he stayed silent and still.

The box Ken was holding was full of Chester's special treat. It was cat chocolate. Good for cats, but not good for little boys.

Chester watched as Ken
gobbled the whole box. He purred
happily.

Tomorrow Ken was going to be a very sick little boy. He would have to go home. Tomorrow everything would be back to normal again.

Chester closed his eyes and went back to sleep. He dreamed of little chocolate boys hopping into his mouth.

Yum!

Kate Darling

Every cat I ever owned was a little bit odd. Some of them were very sweet, and one was really rather nasty! The cat in this story is a bit like a cat I once had, who didn't like it much when people came to visit. He liked to get *all* the attention.

I don't have any pets any more, but there's a skinny brown cat who comes to my back door every night and yowls loudly until I let him in and give him a little bit of chocolate! I'm sure it's not good for him, but it makes him very happy.

Mitch Vane

I think I caught the drawing bug from my mother. I used to watch her draw and paint as I was growing up. She was very good at it.

Now I am an artist too. I do most of my artwork in ink, using a scratchy fountain pen. I am a very messy worker, so my fingers and clothes are *always* covered in ink.

I didn't have a cat to pose for me when I was doing the drawings for this story, but I made Chester a bit like my sister's cat, Puss, who was very grumpy and very spoiled.

jwzels

4|6 991 - 1134

og

831 - 3090

marlon

647 333 6775